Rachel's Day
in the Garden

A Kids Yoga Spring Colors Book

By Giselle Shardlow

Illustrated by Hazel Quintanilla

D1377679

For all young children everywhere who enjoy gardening. ~ G.S.

ISBN-13: 978-1500138493
ISBN-10: 1500138495

Kids Yoga Stories
Boston, MA
www.kidsyogastories.com
www.amazon.com/author/giselleshardlow
Email us at info@kidsyogastories.com

Ordering Information: Special discounts are available on quantity purchases by contacting the publisher at the email address above.

What do you think? Let us know what you think of *Rachel's Day in the Garden* at feedback@kidsyogastories.com

Printed in the United States of America.

How to Use This Kids Yoga Book

Welcome to Kids Yoga Stories. Our yoga books are designed to integrate learning, movement, and fun. Below are a few tips for getting the most out of this spring colors yoga book:

1. **Flip** through this yoga story to familiarize yourself with the format. Pay special attention to the yoga pose in the circle on each page. Each pose has a corresponding keyword.

2. **Read** the story with your child, but this time, act out the story as you go along. Use the illustrations of Rachel doing the poses as a guide. Encourage your child's imagination.

3. **Refer** to the list of kids yoga poses and the parent-teacher guide at the back of the book for further information.

Enjoy your yoga story, but please be safe!

Extended Mountain Pose

"Good morning, world!"
Rachel said as she basked in
the rays of the yellow **sun**.

"Let's go play in the garden, Sammy!" Rachel scooped up her puppy and gave him a hug. The sky was a gorgeous blue.

Standing Forward Bend

Rachel and Sammy skipped around the backyard.

After a while, a light rain began to fall.

Tree Pose

The pair huddled under the green leaves of a tall **tree**. Rachel felt the rain gently sprinkling her face. She took a deep breath and smelled the wet earth.

Warrior
3 Pose

Sammy looked up and tilted his head to listen.

Rachel looked up, too.
A red bird was settling
into its nest.

Then the misty rain stopped.

Rachel remembered that she had pumpkin seeds to **plant** in the garden. She spaced the seeds two inches apart in the brown, wet soil. "I love getting my hands dirty!"

Locust Pose

"Look, Sammy!
An orange **caterpillar**!
Sometimes, caterpillars are
naughty and eat leaves, but
they are still beautiful,"
Rachel said.

Hero
Pose

"Colorful, sweet-smelling flowers like tulips attract yellow **bees**," Rachel said. "Bees help our vegetable garden grow."

Sammy wagged his tail.

Cobbler's Pose

Sammy jumped up and down, trying to catch a fluttering purple **butterfly.**

"Silly Sammy!" Rachel giggled.

"Butterflies love pink **flowers**!"

Rachel said to Sammy.

"That's why we plant zinnias."

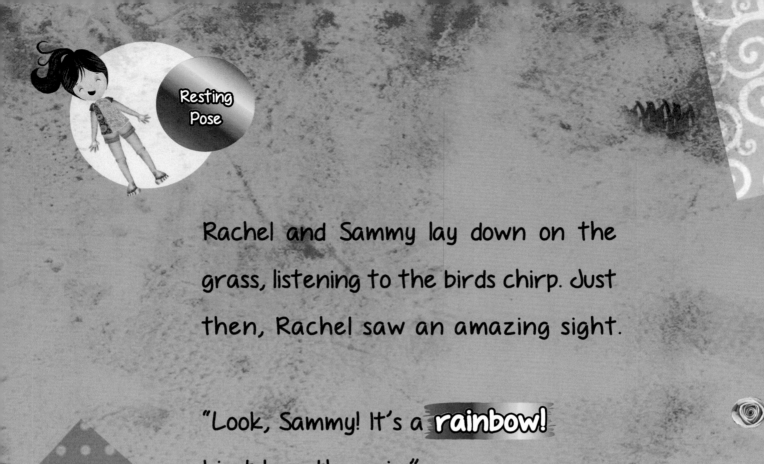

Rachel and Sammy lay down on the grass, listening to the birds chirp. Just then, Rachel saw an amazing sight.

"Look, Sammy! It's a **rainbow!** I just love the rain."

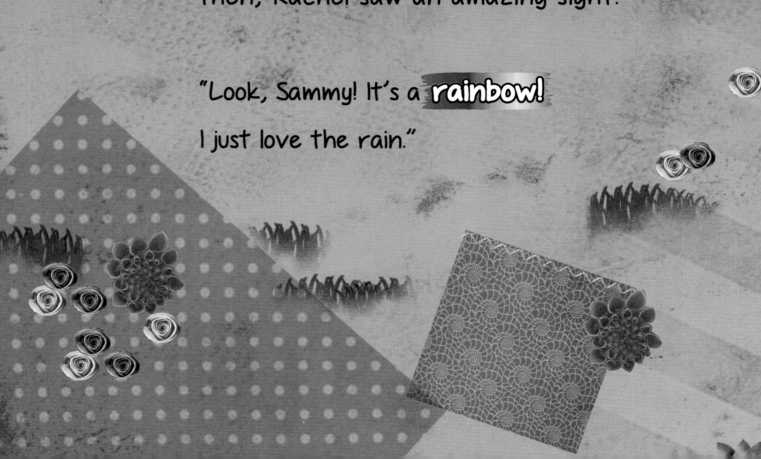

List of Kids Yoga Poses

The following list is intended as a guide only. Please encourage the children's creativity while ensuring their safety.

	Keyword	Yoga Pose	Demonstration
1	Sun	Extended Mountain Pose	
2	Rain	Standing Forward Bend	

	Keyword	Yoga Pose	Demonstration
3	Tree	Tree Pose	
4	Bird	Warrior 3 Pose	
5	Plant	Squat Pose	

	Keyword	Yoga Pose	Demonstration
6	Caterpillar	Locust Pose	
7	Bees	Hero Pose	
8	Butterflies	Cobbler's Pose	

	Keyword	Yoga Pose	Demonstration
9	Flower	Flower Pose	
10	Rainbow	Resting Pose	

Parent-Teacher Guide

This guide contains tips to get the most out of your experience of yoga stories with young children.

Put safety first. Ensure that the space is clear and clean. Spend some time clearing any dangerous objects or unnecessary items. Wear comfortable clothing and practice barefoot. Wait one to two hours after eating before practicing yoga.

Props are welcome. Yoga mats or towels (on a non-slip surface) are optional. Spring-related props and spring-themed music are a good addition.

Cater to the age group. Use this Kids Yoga Stories book as a guide, but make adaptations according to the age of your children. Feel free to lengthen or shorten your journey to ensure that your children are fully engaged throughout your time together. Our recommendation is to read the book with children ages two to five (toddlers to preschoolers).

Talk together. Engage your children in the book's topic. Talk about the keywords or seasons so they can form meaningful connections. Explain the purpose of yoga stories—to integrate movement, reading, and fun.

Learn through movement. Brain research shows that we learn best through physical activity. Our bodies are designed to be active. Encouraging your children to act out the keywords not only allows them to have fun, but also helps them learn about colors and spring. Use repetition to engage the children and help them learn the movements. Ask your child to say or predict the next pose in their garden exploration.

Develop breath awareness. Throughout the yoga session, bring the children's attention to the action of inhaling and exhaling in a light-hearted way. For example, encourage them to make a buzzing sound like a bee. Try staying in the poses long enough to take a few deep breaths.

Relax. Allow your children time to end their session in Resting Pose for five to ten minutes. Massage their feet during or after their relaxation period. Relaxation techniques give children a way to deal with stress. Reinforce the benefits and importance of quiet time for their minds and bodies. Introduce meditation, which can be as simple as sitting quietly for a couple of minutes, as a way to bring stillness to their highly stimulated lives.

Lighten up and enjoy yourself. A children's yoga experience is not as formal as an adult class. Encourage the children to use their creativity and provide them time to explore the postures. Avoid teaching perfectly aligned poses. The journey is intended to be joyful and fun. Your children feed off your passion and enthusiasm. So take the opportunity to energize yourself, as well. Read and act out the book together as a way to connect with each other.

About Kids Yoga Stories

We hope you enjoyed your Kids Yoga Stories experience.

Visit www.kidsyogastories.com to:

Receive updates. For updates, contest giveaways, articles, and activity ideas, sign up for our free Kids Yoga Stories Newsletter.

Connect with us. Please share with us about your yoga journey. Send pictures of you or your little ones practicing the poses or reading the story. Describe your journey on our social media pages (Facebook, Pinterest, Twitter, and Google+).

Check out free stuff. Read our articles on books, yoga, parenting, and travel. Download one of our kids yoga lesson plans or coloring pages.

Read or write a review. Read what others have to say about our yoga books or post your own review on Amazon or on our website. We would love to hear how you enjoyed this book.

Thank you for your support in spreading our message of integrating learning, movement, and fun.

Giselle

Kids Yoga Stories

www.kidsyogastories.com

giselle@kidsyogastories.com

www.pinterest.com/kidsyogastories

www.youtube.com/KidsYogaStories

www.facebook.com/kidsyogastories

www.twitter.com/kidsyogastories

www.amazon.com/author/giselleshardlow

www.goodreads.com/giselleshardlow